Life of a Gay Frat Boy: First Time

Life of a Gay Frat Boy

L. Porter

Published by L. Porter, 2023.

This is a work of fiction. Similarities to real people, places, or events are entirely coincidental.

LIFE OF A GAY FRAT BOY: FIRST TIME

First edition. July 12, 2023.

Copyright © 2023 L. Porter.

Written by L. Porter.

Also by L. Porter

Das Leben eines schwulen Verbindungsjungen
Band 1: Das Leben eines schwulen Verbindungsjungen

Life of a Gay Frat Boy
Volume 1: Life of a Gay Frat Boy
Volume 2: Life of a Gay Frat Boy
Life of a Gay Frat Boy: First Time

Meinen heterosexuellen Mitbewohner verführen
Band 1: Meinen heterosexuellen Mitbewohner verführen
Band 2: Meinen heterosexuellen Mitbewohner verführen

Author's Note

Hi there,

Thanks for reading my story Life of a Gay Frat Boy: First Time! I hope you enjoy it and would appreciate if you'd leave a review after you've finished reading it on the store of your choice.

If you'd like to receive release updates, freebies, and more sign up to my newsletter at www.lporter.sbs.

Happy Reading!

L. Porter

Chapter 1: Plans

<u>Alice</u>

My name is Alice, and I'm feeling unhappy with the state of affairs in my little brother's life. Alex just turned 18 yesterday and as of today, he is still a virgin. If I cornered him into having a conversation about sex, I know he would blush and stammer and claim otherwise but deep down in my heart, I know my brother is still a virgin. Furthermore, I am one hundred percent certain that he is a flamingly gay, take it up the butt, raging homosexual. Though again, if I tried to confront him, he would absolutely deny it to the grave.

Despite my best efforts to encourage him out of his shell, Alex has steadfastly refused to acknowledge he's gay or how to go about actually acting on his attraction. Growing up together I have always known Alex was different, and I've loved him for it. Our parents are oblivious of course, but It's always been obvious to me that he doesn't like girls and was going to eventually have to come out of the closet. I'd thought for sure he would have managed to hook up with a guy during one of the many parties he attended throughout high school, but there has been no luck there. There was a disastrous attempt with a girl, that quickly spread throughout the entire school, and since Alex has been radio silent about dating or romance in general.

I've decided for Alex that this has to stop. Having just turned 18, I'd expected to find my brother out of the closet, going out at all times of the day and night, etc., however that hasn't been the case at all. I'm back home from college for the summer, so this is going to give me lots of ample time to start planning on hooking Alex up. I'm going to make it my mission to get Alex laid.

"Oh Alex, why do you have to make it so hard for yourself sometimes" I mutter out loud, eyes glossed over as I think about the situation. Suddenly a thought comes into my mind, and I chuckle maniacally as a plan begins to form in my head.

"Hmph, well that settles it then. I think I might know just the guy for Alex, and just how I'm going to get him out of his shell" I think, grinning in triumph as I start laying out the foundation for my sinister plan.

***

Alex

I close my locker door, slamming it shut for the last time in his high school career. Shaking my head, I quickly heft up my heavy book bag filled with textbooks and my laptop across my shoulder and began shambling along out the front doors of the school.

I navigate my way through the crowds of teenagers leaving the school, and suddenly jump and stifle a yell as I feel the unexpected touch of a hand drop on my arm and squeeze it tightly startling me. Looking over at the owner of the hand I see my best friend, Damian, laughing at my reaction and stare angrily at him for a moment before smiling back and chuckling at his antics.

Damian is 6 feet tall, brown curly hair, brown eyes, with dark skin that contrasts sharply against his glowing white teeth. He has a smile that could stop hearts if you weren't prepared for it. More than a few of our classmates have fallen for his charms throughout the high school senior year, and he has developed somewhat of a reputation as a womanizer. Even with that reputation though, he's still one of the most likable guys around and I can't help but harbor a small crush on him.

"Dude, you need to stop doing that! You literally could have given me a heart attack." I say in exasperation, for what feels like the millionth time.

"Nah, otherwise how would I get to enjoy seeing you freak out each time I do it? Besides Alex, you need to loosen up a little; you're too wound up all the time. Why don't you live a little?" Damian jokingly replies back, laughing at the look on my face.

"You know I don't like being startled like that, but whatever obviously it's not going to stop you anyway." I say, resigned to this aspect of our friendship.

"Whatever. Anyway, what did you think about your last day in high school? Happy it's over, or sad and filled with ennui at the end of it all?" Damian asks, exaggerating the last words.

I can't help but snort, Damian is a character. "Yeah, I'm so filled with melancholy. Will you be the one to save me?" I say, batting my eyelashes at him and swooning at him as if I'm a damsel in distress.

Damian hams it up, laughing as he swoops me up into his arms pulling me into them and against his broad shoulders and firm muscles. I can feel them through his cotton shirt, and I blush and bury my face into his chest.

"Damian, you know you can be a royal pain in the ass right?" I say, my voice muffled into his shoulder as he carries me bridal style through the parking lot to my car.

"Why I never! Here I am just carrying a damsel in distress to his vehicle, and he insults me." He replied, acting offended while fighting back a smile.

"Right, well you can put the damsel in distress down now" I state, my blush having now faded enough to allow me to reveal my face to Damian without embarrassment.

"As my lady wishes" he states, placing me down by the driver's door and bowing down to me teasingly.

Both of us sit there for a moment, before bursting into laughter at Damian's antics.

"Get in the car, I can drop you off at home. "I say, pointing to the passenger side door.

Damian rushes over to the passenger side, eagerly jumping into the seat and buckling.

"Thanks, a 5 minute drive beats a 20 minute walk home any day of the week" he says, grinning at me.

"No worries" I say, getting in after stowing my bag in the backseat. I quickly start up the car and navigate the parking lot dodging teenagers on their phones.

"So, no joking aside, what are you going to do now that school is done?" Damian asks me, his face turning more seriously.

I sigh, thinking about what I'm going to have to decide this summer. "Well, you know I have to do pre-med. My sister, Alice, chose to go into law and it just about killed my mom and dad. Mom wants me to stay here in Texas, so I can live at home, and she can mother me more." I reply.

"Hmm, that would be like high school again just with a larger college bill to pay on top." Damian pensively replies.

I nod absentmindedly. "Yeah, I don't think I want to do that. You know I can't be myself here, I need to go and spread my wings somewhere else. There's a program in North Carolina I was checking out. It's got good ratings, and the college even offered me a scholarship. I think I could convince my dad to get on board with it, so my mom won't have a choice."

"Well, I'll miss you if you go, but you have to do what's right for you. Besides, I think you need to get out of state so you can get some dick. Your tight virgin ass can't stay that way forever, but if you keep living mama's basement you're not getting laid anytime soon" Damian replies while chuckling.

I snort, unable to control my laughter at his irreverent tone and response.

"Maybe that too" I concede.

I pull up to Damian's house, putting the car into park. He unbuckles his seatbelt, while gathering his bag up from the car floor, and gets out of the car leaving the door open for a moment longer.

"Hey Alex, why don't I take you out tomorrow night? It's your birthday, and I'm pretty sure I can get you into some clubs. My cousin is a bouncer at one of them, so I'm sure I can sneak you in."

I hesitate, thinking about my answer. I'm not usually a big party-person, but you only turn 18 once and this summer is the last chance I'm going to have to hang out with Damian in a long time.

"Uh yeah sure, just text me the club and time later." I say nervously.

Damian's face lights up again, and his smile is back on his face. "Awesome, I'll see you later then" he says, before closing the door and running into his house.

***

Alice

I stare at my phone screen, reading a text from Damian. He performed admirably and got Alex to agree to go to the club tomorrow night. Step 1 of my plan is complete, and now I just have to put step 2 into action. Scrolling through my phone's contacts, I find exactly the guy I'm looking for: Hayden.

Hayden and I go back, he was a year behind me in high school and was one of the few gay guys who was brave enough to be out at the time. He came out when he was in junior high and didn't let anyone mock him for being gay. He even managed to get onto the football team, which made him extremely popular. It probably didn't hurt that he was ridiculously easy on the eyes, standing 6 feet tall with toned muscles and washboard abs. More than a few girls were upset when he came out; he broke a few hearts I'm sure.

Last I checked Hayden was single, and I'm pretty sure he just came back from an epic Europe Trip for a year. The pictures he was posting with men around the continent showed he definitely gets around and gained some experience along the way. Beyond it all, he always struck me as a good guy. He was nice, considerate, and was always a positive presence whenever I was around him. I think he'd be good for Alex and would draw him out of his shell.

Making my decision, I pick up my phone and hit dial. The phone rings for a few seconds, and a masculine voice answers.

"Hello"

"Hey, this is Hayden right?" I ask.

"Um yeah, who is this?" Hayden answers, sounding confused.

"Hey Hayden, it's Alice from high school. You remember me right? We used to sit together in AP English." I reply cheerfully.

The line is silent for a moment, then I hear an intake of breath. "Alice, right, sorry it took me a second. How's it going? We haven't talked in a while."

"Yeah totally, it's great. I just got back from my first year at college, and wanted to know if you wanted to hang out? I saw from your post that you're back in town."

"Sure, I could chill; what did you have in mind?" he replies, sounding nonchalant.

"Great, well my brother just turned 18 and I was going to go with him and his friend to the clubs tomorrow night. Do you want to join and help us loosen him up a little?" I asked, trying to hide the nerves in my voice.

"Your brother's Alex right? I think I remember seeing him at school once or twice." Hayden asked with an intrigued tone to his voice.

I stifle a squeal as I realize he's interested in Alex; this couldn't have turned out more perfect! "Yes, Alex is my little brother. He just turned 18 and we need to get him out of the house and having some fun. I remember seeing you being the life of the party in high school; I'm sure you could distract him. "I reply, playing dumb at the obvious interest in his voice.

"Totally, send me the club address and time and I'll meet you guys there tomorrow. I'm looking forward to seeing you and your brother again!" Hayden replies eagerly.

"Great, see you tomorrow." I say, before hanging up the phone. I can't help myself but let out a little scream of joy, flinging myself back onto my bed. This is it, phase 2 of my plan is complete!

Chapter 2: The Club

Alex

I'm anxiously wandering around my bedroom fidgeting with my clothes, trying to find the right outfit for tonight. I'm usually more of a jeans and t-shirt kind of guy, but I want to dress up nice for tonight. Damian is taking me out, and it turns out he invited Alice along as well.

I'm not upset about Damian inviting Alice; I don't really get to see my big sister much and she is a lot of fun to hang out with. I'm sure she will be the life of the party and make it even better for me. She loves me, and growing up together she seemed to know what I needed before I even knew. Whatever happens tonight, I'll feel safer having her around anyway.

I frantically fly through my closet, searching for anything to where, but I just can't make up my mind. Giving up, I decide to bring out the big guns.

"Alice, I need your help!" I yell out my bedroom door, in the direction of Alice's bedroom.

"Coming" I hear yelled back from behind her closed door, and I move back into my bedroom flopping back onto my bed with my hands over my face moaning in despair.

Alice bounces into the room, full of energy and excitement. She's a 5 foot 6 inch bundle of energy, with a pixie cut and the attitude to match. She's the kind of person where she's either your best friend or your worst enemy; not someone to be trifled with on the best of days. I once made the mistake of stealing her cookie when I was 7, and she framed me for the ruthless murder of one of her stuff animals. My dad grounded me for 3 weeks for my "crime" because of her; I learned very quick to stay on her good side after that.

"You called?" Alice says chipperly, taking in my depressed and frantic demeanor.

"Yes, I don't think I can do this. I don't have anything to wear, and I'm nervous, and honestly I think I might be coming down with the flu." I rant, becoming incoherent with panic.

"Okay then brother dearest, let's take a chill pill and try breathing. Firstly, you have lots to wear. I'll help you pick it out myself, and you will be stunning. Secondly, don't you dare chicken out on me, or I will string you up by your guts myself. You are going out tonight and that is final! Are we understood?" Alice asked, voice sweet and in no way matching the tone she had just used to cajole and threaten me.

"Yup, crystal clear" I say, leaping from my bed and back to my feet in terror of my ruthless sister.

"Excellent. Now then, let's go about making you the sexiest little twink in the club!" Alice exclaims, turning away to peruse my closet.

"Alice, seriously stop calling me that. Mom might hear you!" I say frantically, in hushed tones in case my mother is nearby.

Alice stops what she is doing and turns around to face me with a menacing glare on her face. "Let's get this straight: I know you're gay and I don't care. I've known since you were literally in grade school, and I'm sure Mom and Dad know somewhere deep down inside as well. You seriously need to grow up and get out there. We are not going to continue ignoring who you are, and I'm not beating around the bush with you anymore. Got it?"

I swallow nervously, then nod. "Okay." I reply weakly.

Alice softens, her eyes looking warmer. "I love you little bro, and we are going to make a man out of you tonight. Now, let's get back to the mission at hand. Finding you a deliciously fuckable outfit!"

I can't help but squeak hearing her say it out loud, but part of me likes what she is saying as well. I brace myself and move toward the closet and Alice who already has a stack of clothing set aside for me to try on. Leaning down, I grab the shirt on top of the pile and start stripping.

***

**Alice**

We pull up to the club I've selected, and I'm feeling smug looking over at Alex who is nervously fidgeting in the passenger seat beside me. After nearly two hours of costume tryouts and selection and near constant embarrassed whining from him, I selected a winning outfit that I am incredibly proud of. Alex is wearing a skin adhering pair of black cotton pants, contouring to his slender legs and perky bubble butt. The pants are complimented by a flashy button up collared shirt, with tastefully elegant floral designs on a dark background. I insisted he leave the buttons only half done up, so you can get glimpses of his nipples and skin when the wind blows across his chest.

Moving up to the face and hair, I helped clean up his hair and trimmed it up into a neatly manicured yet wild look. I also helped him with some minimal makeup, just to contour things and applied a small amount of eye liner to bring out his gorgeous eye color. He honestly looks drop dead sexy, and part of me wonders if Hayden isn't going to have some competition for my brother tonight.

"Did Damian say when he was going to meet us here?" Alex asks anxiously, looking around through the car windows for him.

"He said he'd be here right around 9, so I'm sure he's just waiting by the doors for us. He said he had a connection to get you into the club, right?" I reply calmly, trying not to make Alex more nervous.

"Yeah he said his cousin was the bouncer." Alex says, still looking around to find Damian. His face lights up with a smile, and I see Damian waving at us from by the door. He's standing next to a large, tall, musclebound man wearing a black shirt by the entrance; presumably the club bouncer cousin.

We both jump out of the car, and Alex runs over to greet Damian happily. Damian laughs seeing him approach and wraps Alex up in a big hug with his arms holding Alex tightly. I shake my head, sighing at the idiocy of men sometimes. It's pretty clear that these two are overly affectionate, and eventually both of them are going to end up in bed together. Until then though, Alex will just have to go along with my master plan.

I hear a masculine cough behind me and turn around to find Hayden walking up the sidewalk towards us. He smiles as he recognizes me.

"Hey Alice, it's so great to see you" he says, wide smile on his face.

"Hayden, I'm so happy you could make it!" I reply genuinely jumping up and down and quickly giving him a warm hug.

Hayden laughs at my reaction and pulls away after a moment to inspect me. "You're looking good these days; seems like college is treating you well."

I laugh, appreciating the compliment. "Thanks, yeah college is great and the guys in California are just sublime. Then again, I'm sure you know all about that!" I reply, winking back at him being less than subtle.

He nods back smiling. "I do recall a very nice two weeks spent on the beach with quite a few washboard abs on surfer bodies. The men are certainly very welcoming out there, that's for sure."

"No kidding, it's been fun so far! Anyway, let me introduce my brother Alex and his friend Damian." I reply, stepping aside to gesture toward Alex and Damian who are both standing awkwardly behind me.

Damian is the first to speak, walking up confidently and holding out his hand for Hayden to shake. "Hey man, nice to meet you! Alice mentioned she was bringing a friend tonight, but it's nice to meet you in person."

Hayden politely replies, eyes cool and closed off. It seems like he is just humoring Damian by acknowledging him. "Nice to meet you too; I'm sure tonight is going to be fun for all of us."

Alex begrudgingly follows suit, shyly approaching Hayden and waving a greeting. "Hi, Alice didn't tell me she was bringing a friend." I quickly intervene, smoothing things over. "Sorry I meant to tell you about it, but it totally slipped my mind. Hayden and I went to school together; he was on the football team in his senior years when you started at the school."

Alex looks like he's thinking for a moment, trying to recall who Hayden is. His eyes widen, and I can tell that he's made the connection and recalls exactly who I'm talking about now. I can also see that Alex had a crush on Hayden at the time, as Alex has started blushing.

Hayden steps up, warmly greeting Alex. "Hey Alex, I'm Hayden. Sorry about Alice; she mentioned it was your birthday and I thought I'd come out and help show you a good time. If you're okay with it that is?" Hayden pauses for a moment, gazing at Alex with a warm expression on his face and open body language.

Alex is still blushing, and I can see he is shy still, but I can also sense an undercurrent in his eyes. He looks intrigued by Hayden, and the two seem to be having some form of silent communication with one another physically.

"Sure, you can buy me my first drink" Alex says finally, relaxing and smiling at Hayden.

"Excellent, just what I wanted to hear! Let's go make this a night you won't forget" Hayden replies, smirking slightly and looking satisfied with himself. He grabs Alex's hand and starts leading him into the club. Damian's bouncer cousin smiles at us, and waves us in without checking ID, as Damian promised he would.

I can't help but chuckle to myself; it's clear my plan is working out exactly as intended. Alex is clearly interested in Hayden, and Hayden appears to have taken an interest in Alex as well. From here on out, I should be able to sit back and let things unfold naturally.

***

Alex

I'm on the dance floor of the club, with the music beating and shaking through me. Hayden is at the bar, ordering me a drink. Alice and Damian are nearby, dancing with each other laughing while surreptitiously watching Hayden and I.

I never really had a chance to meet Hayden in high school, but I knew who he was. Part of me envied him for his ability to be genuine and authentic to himself, though it was something I wanted I never felt able to with my parents around. Something about Hayden is disarming, and I can't help but feel flattered at the attention he is giving me.

Hayden comes back to me carrying a tray with eight shots and a happy smile on his face.

"Here, drink it up Birthday boy. This will do you some good!" he says, handing me one of the shots after setting the tray on a nearby standing table. "Ready, 3...2...1... go!" Hayden says eagerly.

We both down our shots, and I'm surprised at the flavour. It's sweet with a warm aftertaste, and I feel it sliding down my throat pleasantly. I reach over and grab another, Hayden matching me, and quickly down it as well. We both down the rest of the shots, and Hayden grabs me hand and starts leading me to the dance floor as a new song starts.

"Come on, let's dance already. You'll feel the buzz from those shots in a few minutes anyway."

Hayden and I dance to the beat of the music, a bass heavy electronic song playing loudly from the speakers, as the booze hits me, and I start to feel pleasantly relaxed. Hayden looks to be in about the same state of mind and is laughing as we dance together. Hayden's eyes are roaming over my body as we dance, and it feels like they are carving trails across me. I can see he's interested in me, and I'm reciprocating his feelings.

His well defined muscles are clear through the shirt he's wearing, and his pants emphasize his bulge prominently. My eyes gaze down and linger on it, noting how his pants accentuate his cock and help me imagine what I might find underneath them. I can faintly see the outline of his dick pushing up against his pants, the swell of a mushroom head and the long outline of the shaft straining against the zipper. The sight of it makes my mouth water with desire, and I can't help but lick my lips thinking about it. Hayden sees me staring at his bulge, and smirks back knowingly.

At first we're further apart, but as the alcohol kicks in I start to feel bolder and move in a little closer to him until our faces are closer. I wrap my arms around his neck and lean in, placing my head against his chest hearing his heart beating under my ear. We move in tandem with the beat, zoning out the rest of the world around us as we start to entwine and become more familiar with each other. Hayden's hands roam across my shoulders and back, lighting fires under my skin as his finger tips linger across my body.

They move further down, stretching to grip onto my ass. He firmly holds onto each ass cheek over my pants, kneading and pulling on them, teasing me. The feeling has me drunk on arousal, and I can't help but moan into his chest as his hands hitch under my waistband, and fingertips slide beneath my pants and boxers to caress the bare skin on my bubble butt.

I give up control and look up beseechingly into Hayden's eyes. He matches my gaze, lowering his face down and crashing his lips passionately against mine. His mouth is bold, and his tongue swirls around mine in a battle of struggles. Against his passionate embrace, I feel myself swoon and submit to his dominant masculine force and let him control me.

Hayden's fingers continue to wander, edging closer and closer to my crack as he explores my body on the dance floor. Around us, couples are dancing oblivious to what we are doing, and the thought arouses me more, making my dick grow hard against Hayden's front. I can feel Hayden's arousal clearly through his pants, and I can't help but slide my hand down to cup his engorged member through them. The feeling is almost too much for my brain to comprehend, and my mind feels like a whirlwind of emotions.

It feels like I'm not myself as I feel my hand move with a mind of its own, slowly unzipping his pants and sliding in to feel his erection straining against his underwear. My hand continues its journey, slipping into his boxers to grasp onto his erect shaft. I can feel his curly pubic hair brushing up against my fingers, and the veins bulging from his thick cock under my fingers. My fingers glide across it, moving towards the tip of his cock. I can feel the slickness under the glans, precum leaking out at my touch; evidence of his arousal and desire for me.

I moan as I feel Hayden's fingers slip into my crack and feel the pad of a finger push against my tight asshole. My body goes limp at the feeling of the pressure against it, and I feel Hayden supporting me as I go weak in the knees at his touch there. He teases me, pushing into it with his finger and alternating pressure with swirls of it against the surrounding area. Nerve endings are flaring inside of me at his touch, and his finger tips leave trails of fire under my skin as my arousal grows.

As Hayden continues teasing my hole, his lips wander down my cheek and neck. I lean forward, exposing my neck giving him easy access. I feel his tongue move along my neck, sending goosebumps all over my body at his touch. He moves upward, his tongue and lips sucking on my ear, making me stiffen with pleasure and arousal. I moan loudly, the pleasure almost too much to handle as Hayden works my body under his expert hands.

" I think we should get out of here and celebrate your Birthday somewhere more private. What do you think?" Hayden whispers into my ear, his lips moving sensuously against it distracting me with arousal.

"Mhm, yeah I think we should to" I quickly reply, brain fogged with arousal and the feeling of Hayden's hard cock pushing against mine and his fingers pressing into my tight hole overwhelming my senses.

Hayden pulls away, his hands sliding out of my pants suddenly making me miss the presence of his skin against mine. He holds out his hand, and my fingers slip into his, and pulls me out of the club. I blush and wave quickly at Alice and Damian as we pass by them, who have been dancing together a short distance away. Alice looks highly amused, flashing thumbs up signs at me while Damian seems to be pouting about something but still smiles at me as we leave.

***

Alice:

I watch as Alex gets led away by Hayden, and gleefully smile and wave as I see my plan come to fruition. I knew Hayden and Alex would hit it off and feel vindicated knowing my plan was a complete success. I flash a thumbs up to Alex, who blushes but waves back before being rushed out of the club by a Hayden who clearly has plans to break his ass in as soon as they get back to his place.

Damian is beside me, and I look over noticing the frown on his face. He seems upset, and I quickly connect the dots as to why he isn't too happy watching Alex being led away by another guy.

"Damian, if you really wanted to do something with Alex all you'd have to do is talk to him." I say, trying to be supportive.

"What, no it's not like that!" He exclaims, denying it vehemently with hands in the air.

I glare at him for a moment, as he shrinks back at my expression.

"Cut the crap. We both know you have had the hots for Alex for a long time and have been too chicken shit to act on it." I reply angrily.

Damian hangs his head in defeat for a moment, before replying. "Okay fine, yeah I'd rather it had been me taking him home tonight. Obviously that's not happening now though."

I shrug back, content to confirm my suspicious about Damian. "Not tonight no, but Hayden isn't going to be around for anything serious anyway. That is a one night fling or fuck buddies at best. If you want to be with Alex, you're going to have to step up and show him you're interested."

Damian looks back pensively, then nods his head firmly back at me. "Okay, message received."

"Great, now let's go back and dance!" I exclaim, distracting the sulking boy from his melancholy and dragging him back to the dance floor.

Chapter 3: First Time

Alex

After a quick ride home in the back seat of a taxi, we arrive at Hayden's apartment. The ride back is spent entwined with one another in the back seat, our lips smacking and tongues tangling as we explore each other. Awkwardly thanking the driver and paying for the ride, Hayden and I stumble out of the taxi and head inside his apartment building, intermittently stopping to ravish each other's lips as we make our way through the hallways.

We reach Hayden's apartment door, with Hayden pinning me against it as he nuzzles on my neck and grinds his erection against mine. He shakily pulls out his apartment key and unlocks the door before opening it, causing both of us to tumble into the apartment and fall onto the ground. I manage to twist and fall onto Hayden's chest cushioning my fall on his muscular torso. We both take a moment to laugh at ourselves, the movement triggering more friction between our bodies bringing us back to our arousal and erections pressing against each other.

Hayden kicks the door closed with his foot, which is propped behind the door from our fall, and quickly flips me over so that I'm pinned under him. He leans down over me, looking like a Greek god of sex, as his lips ravage mine and I feel his tongue caress mine and teeth catch on my lips tenderizing them. He trails kisses down my neck, reaching my sensitive collarbone making me gasp in pleasure. His hands slide down, roughly ripping open my shirt causing buttons to fly everywhere and slides down to trail kisses down my chest. The sensitive skin flares red with arousal where he touches, and his lips find my tender nipples.

At first he is gentle, suckling on them lightly and teasing them with his tongue. I moan in appreciation, the delicate nubs of flesh giving me flashes of pleasure as he teases them. His tongue becomes more insistent, and he starts to lightly bite at them with his teeth causing sharp flashes of pleasure and pain intermingled with one another. The mixture is overwhelming, and my erection grows harder making my pants feel so tight against it. I whine and try to pull away, the sensations overwhelming me and making me feel light headed.

I hear a chuckle from Hayden, as he holds me in place and continues to tease me with his mouth on my nipple. "You're not getting away that easy. I'm going to show you how good it feels to be used by a man. By the time tonight is done, you are going to be an expert at taking my dick and pleasuring a man." He says, his tone heavy with lust.

My mouth goes dry at his tone, and I feel my tight virgin hole quivering in anticipation of what he is going to do to me. I feel overwhelmed with lust as Hayden tells me how he is going to use me and break in my tight ass for his pleasure. All I can do is nod in response, clearing my throat to try and speak.

"I want you to use me and teach me. Tell me what I need to do to please you. I want you to fuck me and make me your bitch." I say, feeling submissive and ready to be myself with Hayden.

Hayden starts moving further down, his lips teasing my skin as he follows my treasure trail of light hair down my abdomen. My breathing picks up pace as I feel his tongue and lips glide along the skin, edging closer to my groin. Hayden's hands move down, unbuttoning my pants and pulling them off of me with my boxers included in one motion exposing my bare skin to the cool air.

Hayden leans back a moment to admire me naked, licking his lips in appreciation of what he sees. "Damn, you have got a beautiful ass on you. I can't wait to tear that up. That cock looks delicious too." He says, biting his lip in anticipation.

Hayden quickly rips his shirt off, exposing the muscles I was feeling earlier while dancing, and unbuttons his pants pulling them off with his underwear as well. His long fat cock flops out of his pants, exposing what has to be at least 10 inches long and 4 inches wide. Hayden has the cock of a porn star, the skin bulging with veins, topped with a cut mushroom head dripping with juicy precum. It's both incredibly arousing and intimidating all at the same time.

Hayden sees me staring with a mixed look of anticipation, and shock and moves to reassure me. "It looks big but trust me when I say it feels so good when it's inside you pounding away at your G-Spot. You're a virgin right?" He says, sitting back for a moment to look at me.

I nod back, blushing slightly under his gaze. "Yes, I've been too scared to try anything with anyone at school." I reply, feeling almost ashamed of it.

"Don't worry about it; I thought you might be. I'm actually kind of flattered you're doing this with me, and I'll make sure you remember tonight for the rest of your life." Hayden replies grinning, rubbing his hand along my thigh reassuring me.

"Okay, I trust you." I reply, his reassuringly warm presence making me feel safe.

Hayden leans forward again, his hands, tongue, and lips trailing down my body heading directly toward my dick. His hands cup my balls, squeezing and kneading them gently making my breath quicken and causing me to spread my legs wider for him to gain easier access. His lips touch the tip of my cock, and I my body jerks in shock as I feel the edge of his tongue flick out and lap against the underside of my swollen head.

It's all I can do to hold back my moans as he begins suckling at my cock, nursing it tenderly with his lips and tongue. He continues this for a moment, torturing me with his light movements and teasing me as I feel my arousal build with no escape. It's the first time I've really been touched in this way before, and Hayden is teasing me knowing that it's building up the sexual tension within me.

Hayden starts lowering himself further down, his lips stretching around my cock and working the shaft. His hand flutters up and down the shaft, in tandem with his strained lips, as his tongue swirls around my shaft and head. I moan, eyes rolling back as the pleasure of what he is doing to me overtakes me.

"Oh shit, that feels so good Hayden." I moan, enraptured with him and the feeling of his tongue wrapped around my cock.

Hayden continues sucking on my cock, alternating rhythm between fast and slow, edging me along towards oblivion. Each time I get close to cumming, he slows down or stops giving me time to recover before resuming his pace. I become more frantic, fighting the desperation of being on the edge of cumming but not being allowed to by the dominant top who is toying with my body.

"Please Hayden, please let me cum now. " I beg, after what feels like the dozenth time he has stopped while I'm on the edge of releasing my load down his throat.

Hayden smiles and chuckles at the look of desperate need on my face and latches his lips and mouth back onto my cock. He starts sucking hard, his head bobbing up and down rapidly as he takes all of my cock into his mouth and throat. I feel my orgasm approaching and warn him that I'm going to lose control soon.

"Oh, shit Hayden, I'm going to cum soon if you don't stop."

Hayden doesn't slow down, but instead picks up pace as his mouth and tongue works my cock at a feverish pace. I feel my orgasm building as the pressure grows inside me, and all I can do is scream out as I explode shooting wave after wave of cum inside Hayden's mouth and down his throat. He keeps sucking, lapping up every last bit of cum leaking out of me and swallowing every drop. I feel weak as the orgasm leaves me seeing stars, and it takes a minute for me to regain my composure enough to look up at Hayden.

Hayden has a wide smirk on his face and looks proud of himself.

"Orgasm good?" he asks.

"Um yeah, that was amazing. You obviously know what you're doing." I reply, chuckling at the proud expression on his face.

"Thanks, I've had a lot of practice. I met a guy in Paris who was my teacher of sorts, and he insisted I practice every day while I was there. It just so happened he wanted the practice to be done on him; not that I was complaining." Hayden says matter of fact-ly.

Hayden gets up and moves closer to me as he pulls me up to my knees. "Now that you've had your orgasm, it's time for my first one. I'm going to teach you to suck dick the right way, so you can please the next man that uses you after me."

I quickly move my body up so my face is level with Hayden's throbbing cock. Looking at it head on, I can see that he is now leaking precum profusely and it has been dribbling down the underside of his head and shaft and has coated his massive balls. His pubic hair is glistening with the slick precum, and I can smell the musky scent of it as I move closer.

I can't help myself but lean in, nuzzling my nose and face into his crotch. His scent fills my senses, and my arousal grows again as I start to lap at the precum on his balls. The flavour is salty and fills my mouth, and I feel my cunt tremble in response to the taste of it. I've always imagined what another man's precum would taste like, but it's so much more sensual and erotic tasting it in real life.

Hayden watches me lap up his precum, patiently smiling down at me. "That's a good boy, eat it all up now." He says dominantly, making me feel like I've just been rewarded for good behavior as I look up at him.

I move up from his balls, my tongue running along his shaft. I carve circles around it as I try to wrap my tongue around it, but it's too thick for me to fully reach around with my tongue. Even with my hand around the base of thick veiny shaft, my fingers barely meet or touch due to his girth. My tongue and lips reach the bottom of his cut head, and I swirl my tongue into the slit of his cock sucking up the last of his precum. Above me Hayden moans in appreciation, his hands shifting to the back of my head grasping onto my hair like handles.

"Good boy, now suck my fat cock like a good little whore" He orders me, his voice gruff.

I comply meekly, opening my mouth wide to accommodate his fat mushroom head which is even bigger now as its engorged with arousal. My lips stretch as I struggle to take it in, and I force myself to move further down to take it in and get to his long shaft. I'm struggling to breathe around his fat cock as it fills my mouth, and I can feel the bulging veins on his dick pushing against my lips and the tightness of my hot wet mouth. I force myself to take more of his cock, until I'm halfway down on it and I feel it hit the back of my throat.

My eyes are weeping as I struggle to take more and fight my gag reflex to swallow more of his cock. Above me I hear Hayden moaning and saying my name as he watches me impale my throat on his cock.

"That's it Alex, you're a good boy for sucking that cock like that. Let me help you with it." He says, as his hands that are holding my hair push my head further down on his cock. I fight the urge to resist or gag as I feel his cock begin to slide down my throat, water running from my eyes as I will myself to be a good little whore for Hayden. Finally, after a moment, I feel my nose nestle into his pubic hair and look up with eyes streaming at Hayden who is looking down at me with evident pleasure.

"Look at that, doesn't that feel good. Don't you like it when I use your throat like that?" He asks.

"Mhm" I answer back, unable to say anything as my mouth and throat are full of his long fat cock and I can't breathe. Hayden holds my head down on his manhood for another half a minute, as I struggle to breathe, and my vision starts to fade from lack of oxygen.

Finally, Hayden releases his hold on me, and I pull off of his cock with a popping sound as the air seal is broken and I can breathe. I quickly take a breath in again, and without hesitation plunge my mouth and throat back down on his cock. I start bobbing my head and down on it, working the shaft with my hand at the same time swallowing all of it rhythmically. Now that I've swallowed all of his cock, it feels easier to take it all and I feel like I know what I'm doing.

"Look at that, my little slut is learning how to suck dick. You're doing so well, we might have to move onto you taking this cock up your tight ass. Do you want me to fuck your tight cunt and rip you open?" Hayden asks, leering down at me as I work his cock with my mouth, tongue, throats, and lips like a good little submissive bottom should.

I stop to answer him. "Yes, I want you to fuck my tight ass and use it like it's yours." I answer breathlessly, trying to catch my breath from the hard work of sucking his long fat cock.

Hayden nods back and pulls me up to my feet. He quickly leads me over to the nearby couch, and motions for me to get on it.

"Get on all fours, I want you to stick your tight ass out for me so I can use it." He orders firmly, impatiently waiting for me to do as he says.

I scramble to follow his orders and position myself with my bubble butt hanging out over the edge of the couch with me resting my weight on my hands and knees. I look back and see Hayden looking down at my tight pucker, licking his lips in anticipation.

Hayden kneels down behind me, and I feel his hot breath ghost against the delicate skin surrounding my quivering hole. I feel a tentative nudge of something warm, and then Hayden's hot warm tongue is pushing against the tight ring of muscle with no hesitation. His tongue gyrates against it, rhythmically poking against it and alternating patterns. I moan and cry as the sensitive nerve endings in my ass flare with pleasure and push my face down into a nearby pillow.

"Oh, fuck Hayden, yeah eat my tight ass out it feels so good" I try to say, though I'm incoherent and drunk on pleasure and the feelings Hayden is making me experience. I'm not sure how much he gets from the wall of noise I make, but he seems to take it as praise as he dives in harder with his tongue and starts punching it inside me past my tense ring of muscle.

His tongue relaxes my tight ring, letting him push it deeper inside me and I feel weak in the knees as he eats me out and rims my tight ass. After a few more minutes of him making me feel like jelly, he pulls away. I almost complain about the absence of his warm tongue inside me then I feel a finger quickly shove inside me.

I cry out in a mixture of pleasure and pain at the feeling of something intruding inside me, then suddenly moan as Hayden's finger starts twitching methodically and grazes against my prostate causing what feels like a bolt of lightning to stab through me. His finger delves deeper inside me and is supplemented by another that just slides inside me like it was meant to be there. Hayden's fingers slam in and out of me, pushing against all the right curves inside me and applying pressure in all the right places making me a gibbering wreck as I moan and cry and beg for him to go harder.

"Oh god, harder please fuck me harder" I cry, pushing my ass back trying to get his fingers inside me deeper searching for the feeling of fullness I'm desperately craving. I hear Hayden breathing heavily behind me, as one hand has three fingers shoved inside me ramming in and out with reckless abandon, while the other is wrapped around his cock jerking off at the sight of me writhing under him.

Hayden withdraws his fingers, causing me to cry as I feel them slide out of me and leave me feeling empty. He stands up behind me, and his cock is already slick with precum and lube he grabbed from beside the couch.

"Are you ready for me to fuck you?" He asks, eyes bearing deep into mine demanding my submission.

"Yes, fuck me rough. I need that fat cock tearing me open now! Break my tight ass in and teach me how to take a cock" I almost yell, frantic with desire from Hayden's teasing so far.

Hayden nods and moves closer, rubbing his erection along my crack. The feeling of his hot mushroom head pushing against my crack and hole makes me feel dizzy with arousal, and I can't think straight as the essence of my being is centered on the sensation of Hayden's cock pressed up against me. Right now, there is nothing more I want in the world than for that cock to be thrusting inside me.

I feel Hayden's cock linger on my hole, and he starts pushing it inside of me. Even with his loosening me up before with his fingers and tongue, it's tight and I cry in pain as he stretches my tight ring wide open and forces his thick long veiny cock inside of me. I feel his fat mushroom head stretch me wide open, and my ring pops open around it as he pushes forward. His shaft keeps it open, making me whine as I feel it slide further inside me destroying any resistance inside me.

I'm a mess already, hyperventilating on the couch and whining as I feel his cock rest inside me, and his balls slam up against me as he finishes plunging his dick inside me up to the hilt. Hayden gives me a moment to take his cock, letting it rest inside me until some of the initial pain fades and muscles relax enough for my breathing to slow down.

"That's good, you're doing great. It's all inside you now, so you can relax. You're such a good little whore, soon you're going to be an expert on this" Hayden says behind me, his voice firm yet warm as he praises me.

I can't help but perk up, his praise making me feel like I need to work harder for him and take his dick. Deciding I've spent enough time relaxing, I move my hands back and use them to spread my ass cheeks wider giving Hayden more room to fuck me and get in deeper.

"Please, fuck me into the couch" I say pleadingly, looking back at Hayden with fuck-me eyes.

Hayden responds by starting to move, his cock sliding in and out of me slowly at first but rapidly picking up pace until he is slamming his cock in and out of me recklessly. Each thrust into me hits my G-Spot, causing a stream of precum to drip from my rock hard cock onto the couch beneath me. While each thrust out has me scrambling back desperately, trying to keep his cock inside me for as long as I can.

Hayden alternates his pace, thrusting away all the while pushing me further and further over the edge of insanity. The world around me is irrelevant, all that matter is the feeling of Hayden's cock using me and ripping my hole wide open. A stream of gibberish comes from my mouth, filling the room with sounds that I faintly realize are coming from me, as Hayden grunts and moans above me in appreciation of my tight cunt.

"You've got such a good hole Alex, it's so tight and hot. I want to spend all night breaking you in" He pants, breathing heavily as he uses my hole for his own pleasure.

Hayden's cock keeps plunging inside me, and I can't keep going at this pace without a release. His thrusts plunge against my prostate, and I can feel another orgasm building inside of me as he uses me like a paid whore. I can't hold it in any longer, and I release again, screaming as wave after wave of pleasure hits in tandem with Hayden's thrusts. I shoot jets of hot cum onto the couch and floor beneath us, and my cunt spasms with each wave.

My cunt tightens up with my orgasm, and Hayden is pushed over the edge as he begins to frantically start slamming into me recklessly plundering my ass for his own pleasure without a care. With a final yelled grunt, he smashes his cock deep inside me and collapses on top of me pinning me down in the hot sticky puddle of my own cum beneath me. I feel him shooting a continuous stream of hot jizz inside me for what feels like a minute straight, as his hot breath reflects off the back of my neck and he kisses the back of my neck.

We lay like that for several minutes, both breathing heavily and trying to recuperate from the orgasm high we are both riding. I twist backyard, my lips seeking Hayden's and we tenderly kiss each other as our tongues swirl in and out of each other's mouths. Finally, Hayden rolls to the side and pulls me up against him. He pulls my sore ass towards him, and we lay with his arm wrapped around my chest and his semi-hard cock pushed up against my crack teasing it as his hot cum slowly leaks out of my gaping cunt.

"Did you enjoy that?" Hayden asks, feeling tense behind me.

"Yes" I respond instantly. "You used me just the way I wanted, and it felt so good."

I can feel Hayden's smirk behind me, even though I'm not looking at him. "Good, let me know when you're ready for round two."

I react in shock, twisting around and groping him to feel if he is already hard again. "You can't be hard already, that's not possible!"

"Oh really" he says, eyebrows quirked mischievously. "What's that you're feeling down there?" He moves his hips provocatively and I hiss as I feel his fully erect member prod at my sore cunt.

"Fine, let's go now then." I say, looking back at him challengingly.

"Be careful what you wish for" Hayden replies, adjusting himself to line his cock up with my trembling hole.

Hayden shoves forward and his cock slides back inside me, no resistance as he stretches it wide open again with ease. I moan into the pillow, feeling it brush up against my G-Spot as he thrusts inside me. This angle is different, and it feels easier to take his cock as he starts thrusting relentlessly inside me. There's no pain, just pleasure, as his cock stretches me open further and uses my cunt for everything its worth.

With each thrust milky white cum leaks out of my cock onto the couch beside me, and I pant and quiver in pleasure as he wrecks my hole and makes me a mess inside and out. His cock hits a new spot inside me, and I keen as he finds a new way to make me see stars, the pleasure of it making me feel drunk on euphoria.

Hayden pushes me over to lay on the couch and climbs on top of me spreading my legs wider to give him access to my gaping cunt. He starts plowing his cock into my ass, slamming into it loudly over and over as he pile drives into me. I cry into the couch with every slamming motion of his body and cock but lay there willingly taking it like a good submissive bottom should. I let him be in charge and use me whatever way he wants to take his pleasure. I'm taking my pleasure from feeling him inside me and hearing him above me moaning and grunting away.

His thrusts become more frantic, and I can feel my orgasm approaching as his nears as well. With a final thrust he slams into me once more and shoots his cum filling my guts with his sperm, which pushes me over the edge and a gush of cum releases from me further coating the couch beneath us in hot sticky jizz. The intensity of my orgasm in combination with Hayden's thrusts inside me are too much, and I pass out from it.

***

Alex:

I step out of the taxi wincing, my ass feeling sore from last night and the six rounds Hayden managed to last before we finally passed out together exhausted and worn out in his bed. Thanking the driver, I limp toward the house and discreetly open the door hoping my family isn't around. It's almost 2 in the afternoon, so hopefully my parents are still at work, and I manage to quickly get in the house without being detected.

Cringing from the soreness, I make my way up the stairs slowly towards my bedroom. Even in spite of the pain, last night was worth it and I smile to myself remembering every round we went. After I passed out, I woke up a few minutes later to the feeling of Hayden holding me close while fucking me on my side again. It was incredibly hot waking up to the feeling of a cock thrusting deep inside you, and I instantly came when I realized what was happening. Hayden made it his mission to make sure I tried every position, and he fucked me in just about every room in his apartment. He let me ride him at one point, though that didn't last long as he didn't like not being in charge and quickly started pounding his cock deep into my guts as I wasn't going fast enough for him.

After a final goodbye this morning, where I swallowed a final hot load for breakfast on my knees, he sent me on my way and proclaimed me ready to be a good little boy for all the other men that would want to fuck me. Being called that turned me on, and I like it even though it could sound demeaning to others. I'm naturally submissive and being praised for a good boy makes me feel so good and makes me want to submit even more.

Finally reaching my bedroom, I open the door to find Alice patiently waiting on my bed for me. She shrieks in excitement as she sees me and runs up wrapping me in a tight embrace with a shit eating grin on her face. Her excitement is contagious, and I can't help but hug her back and smile at her enthusiasm.

"So, tell me all about it! How was last night? Was Hayden good in bed?" She asked excitedly, not giving me a second to relax before badgering me with questions.

"Alice calm down; you're going to pass out if you don't breathe." I tease her. "Last night was great, and Hayden made it amazing. I couldn't have asked for a better first time." I reply, my eyes going glossy as I remember all the different positions he put me in last night.

Alice smiles, calming down as she sees the expression on my face. "I'm glad it was good. I won't ask for details, but I just want to know this one little thing then I'll leave you alone: how many times?"

"Seriously Alice!" I grumble, slightly shocked at her question while blushing.

"Please!" she begs me, giving me puppy eyes.

"Fine...it was 6 times. We were up basically all night." I reply, a small smile sneaking out as I can't help but feel giddy.

Alice squeals in excitement again and jumps up to hug me. "I'm so proud of you! Anyway, I'll leave you alone now. You look like you're going to pass out soon whether I'm here or not!"

Alice leaves the room skipping giddily away, and I laugh at her ridiculous exit. It's pretty clear to me now that she engineered the entire thing with Hayden, but I can't be mad at her about it. Last night was like a dream come true, and it's going to reside in my spankbank for a long time after this.

Yawning, I quickly pull off my clothes and slide under the covers. I reach down and plug my dead phone in, and the screen lights up as the power brings it back to life. I see a message notification from Damian from last night and open it up.

Damian: Hey man, hope you had a good birthday! There's something I want to talk to you about. Text me when you get this message, and we can talk. XX

I smile, reminded of how much Damian cares for me. I put my phone down, turning off the screen. I'll message him later, I think to myself, as I burrow into my pillow. Soon enough, I'm nodding off to dreams of Hayden's thick long cock pummeling into me. That was probably the best birthday present I've ever received from Alice.

Did you love *Life of a Gay Frat Boy: First Time*? Then you should read *Volume 1: Life of a Gay Frat Boy*[1] by L. Porter!

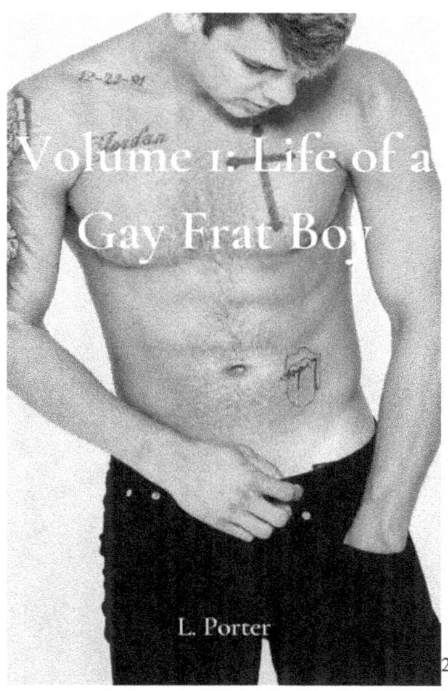

[2]

Alex is an 18 year old Twink who has just left home for the first time. Raised in Texas with an overbearing conservative family, he hasn't been allowed to be the submissive little bottom Twink he has always been inside. He yearns for freedom, and the ability to sleep with any man he wants to.

All that is going to change, now that he is in college far away from home. Alex is determined to express his inner whore, and show the men of North Carolina just how much he can please

---

1. https://books2read.com/u/mK7vQy

2. https://books2read.com/u/mK7vQy

them. To do that, he decides to join the men's fraternity on campus and sample just what true brotherly love means.

www.ingramcontent.com/pod-product-compliance
Lightning Source LLC
Chambersburg PA
CBHW071359200726
48294CB00004B/1225